Christmas is Hell

Russ Haan

Roadside Amusements
an imprint of Chamberlain Bros.
Penguin Group (USA) Inc.
New York
2005

Roadside Amusements
an imprint of Chamberlain Bros.
Published by the Penguin Group
Penguin Group (USA) Inc., 375 Hudson Street, New York, New York 10014, USA
Penguin Group (Canada), 90 Eglinton Avenue East, Suite 700, Ontario M4P 2Y3, Canada (a division of Pearson Penguin Canada Inc.)
Penguin Books Ltd, 80 Strand, London WC2R 0RL, England
Penguin Ireland, 25 St Stephen's Green, Dublin 2, Ireland (a division of Penguin Books Ltd)
Penguin Group (Australia), 250 Camberwell Road, Camberwell, Victoria 3124, Australia
(a division of Pearson Australia Group Pty Ltd)
Penguin Books India Pvt Ltd, 11 Community Centre, Panchsheel Park, New Delhi–110 017, India
Penguin Group (NZ), Cnr Airborne and Rosedale Roads, Albany, Auckland 1310, New Zealand (a division of Pearson New Zealand Ltd)
Penguin Books (South Africa) (Pty) Ltd, 24 Sturdee Avenue, Rosebank, Johannesburg 2196, South Africa

Penguin Books Ltd, Registered Offices: 80 Strand, London WC2R 0RL, England

Copyright©2005 After Hours Creative
All rights reserved. No part of this book may be reproduced, scanned, or distributed in any printed or electronic form without permission. Please do not participate in or encourage piracy of copyrighted materials in violation of the author's rights. Purchase only authorized editions.
Published simultaneously in Canada

An application has been submitted to register this book with the Library of Congress.
ISBN: 1-59609-086-3
Printed in the United States of America
10 9 8 7 6 5 4 3 2 1

Christmas is Hell

Book design and illustrations by After Hours Creative

To my mother, for pretending to put my little brother in the oven.
To my father, for pretending he was hungry.
To Mike, who experiences Hell on a daily basis.

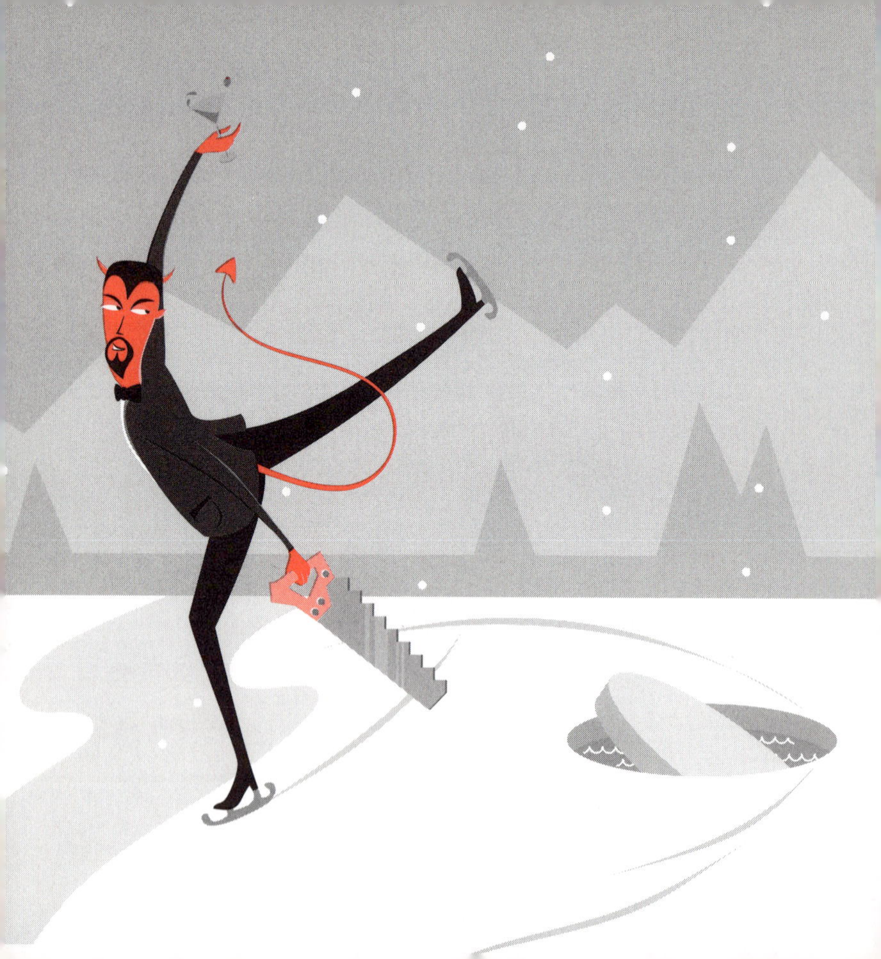

Please do drop in.

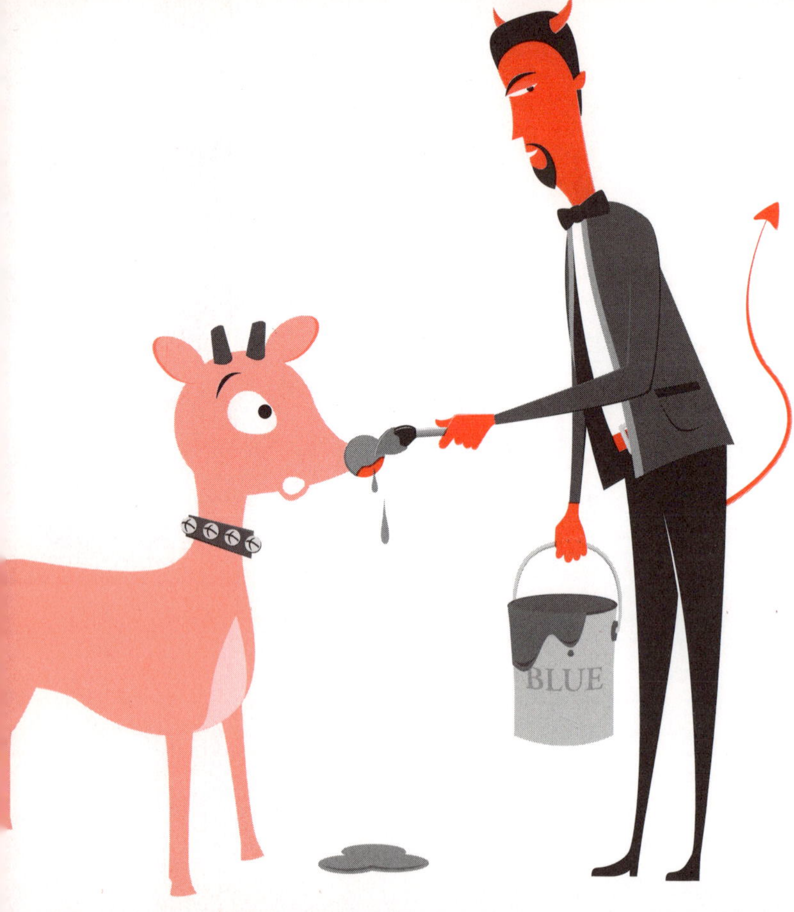
BLUE

Blue is the new red.

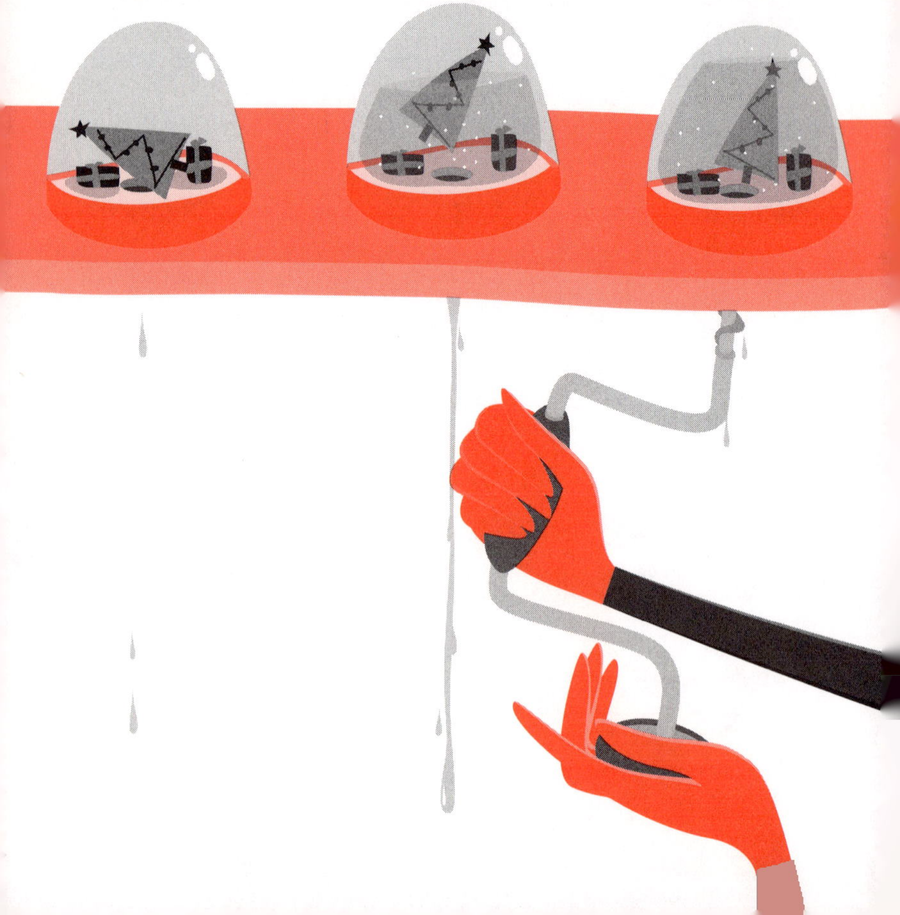

I find the holidays draining.

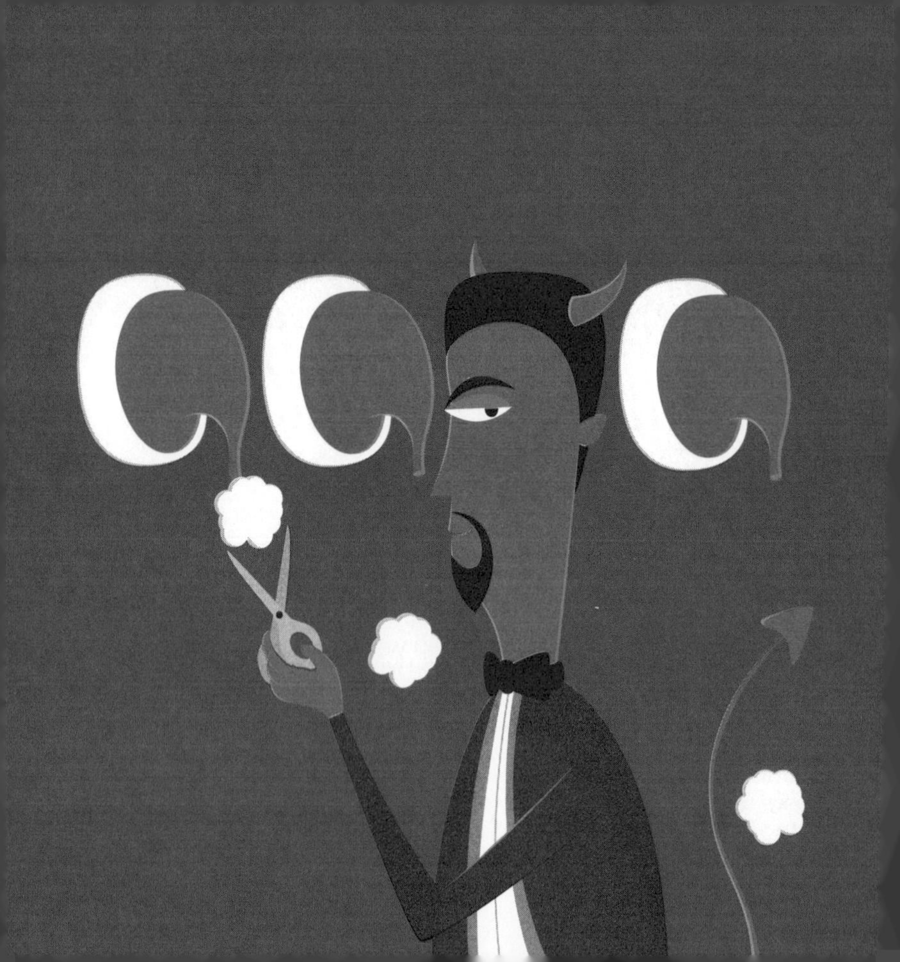

It's Christmas, *
* *have a ball.*

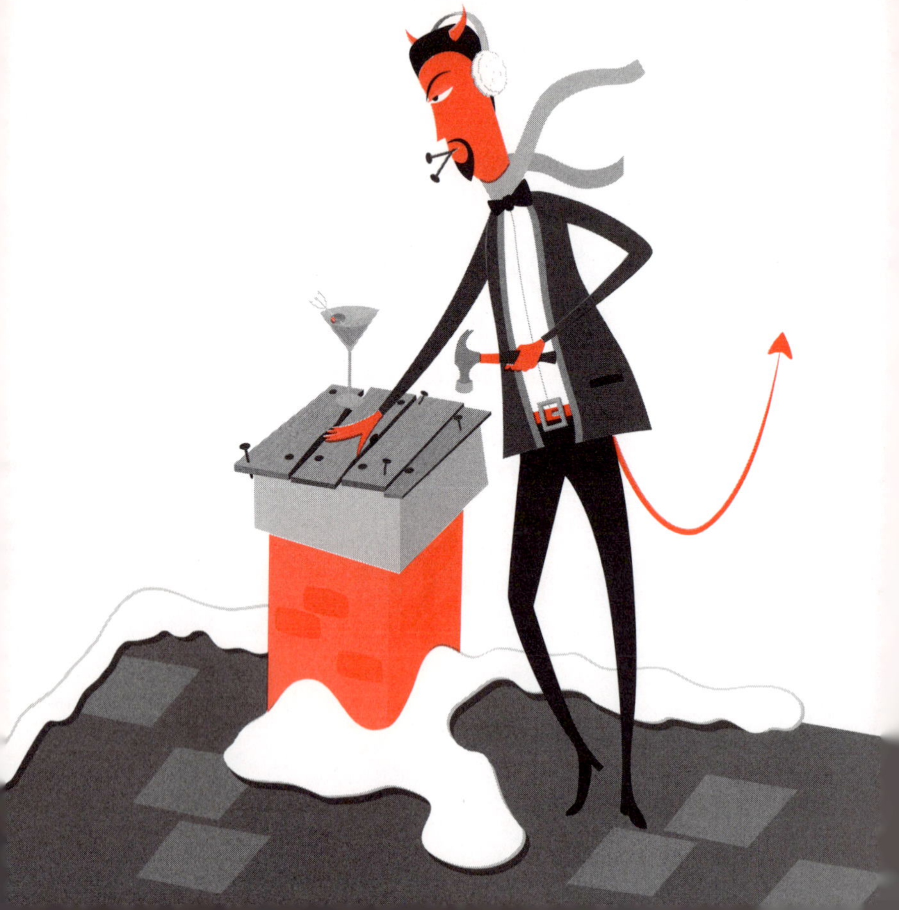

Down through the chimney? I beg to differ.

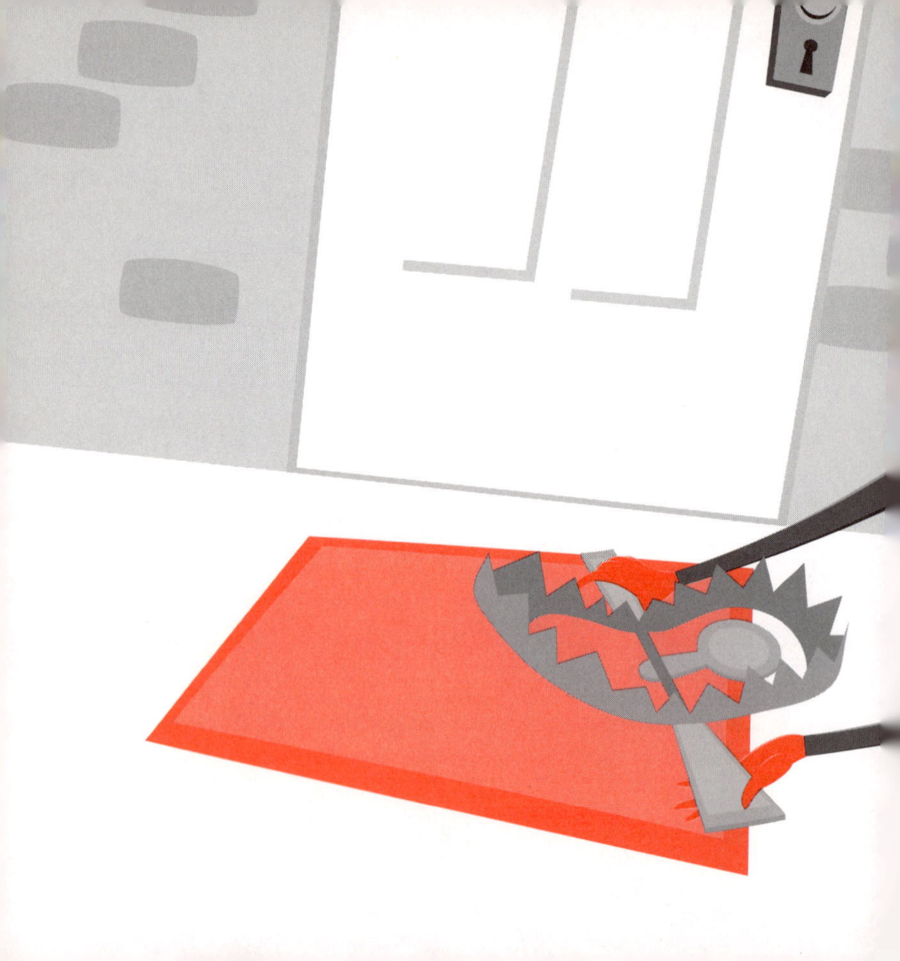

Ah, home for the holidays.

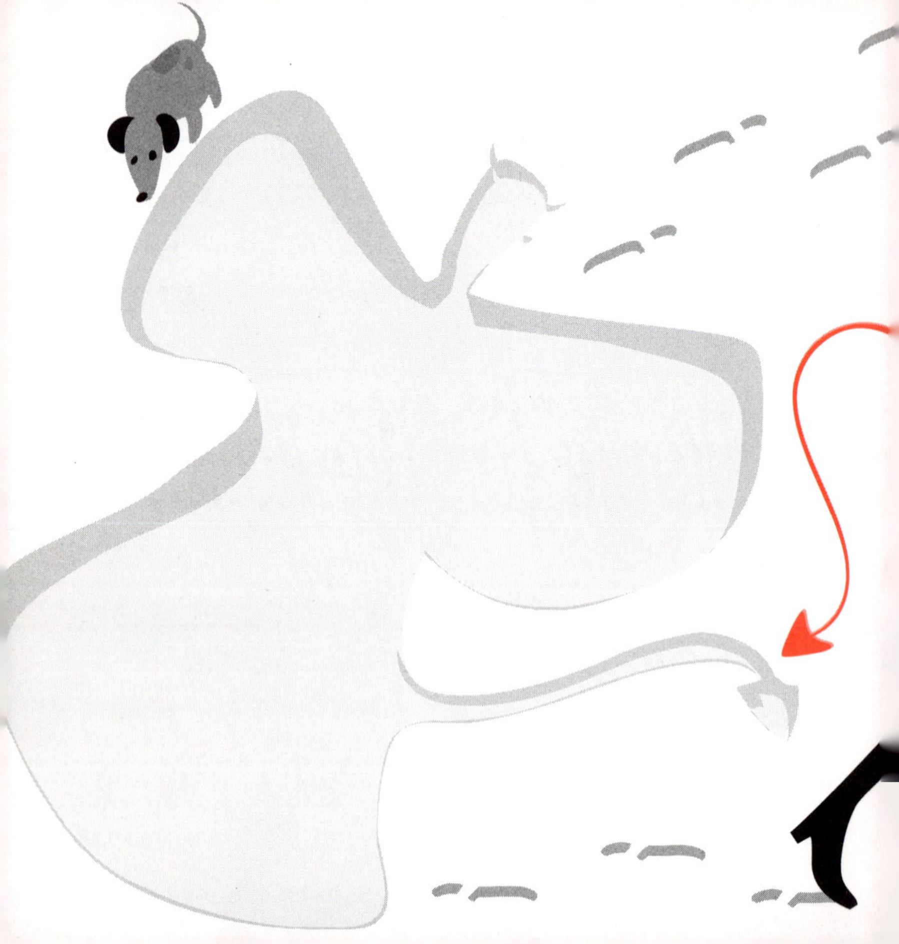

Hark the herald angels singe.

Nice
Naughty
Joanna
Jocelyn
Jodi
Joel
Jonathan
Jordan
Jose
Josephine
Joshua
Joyce

Making a list and checking it twice.

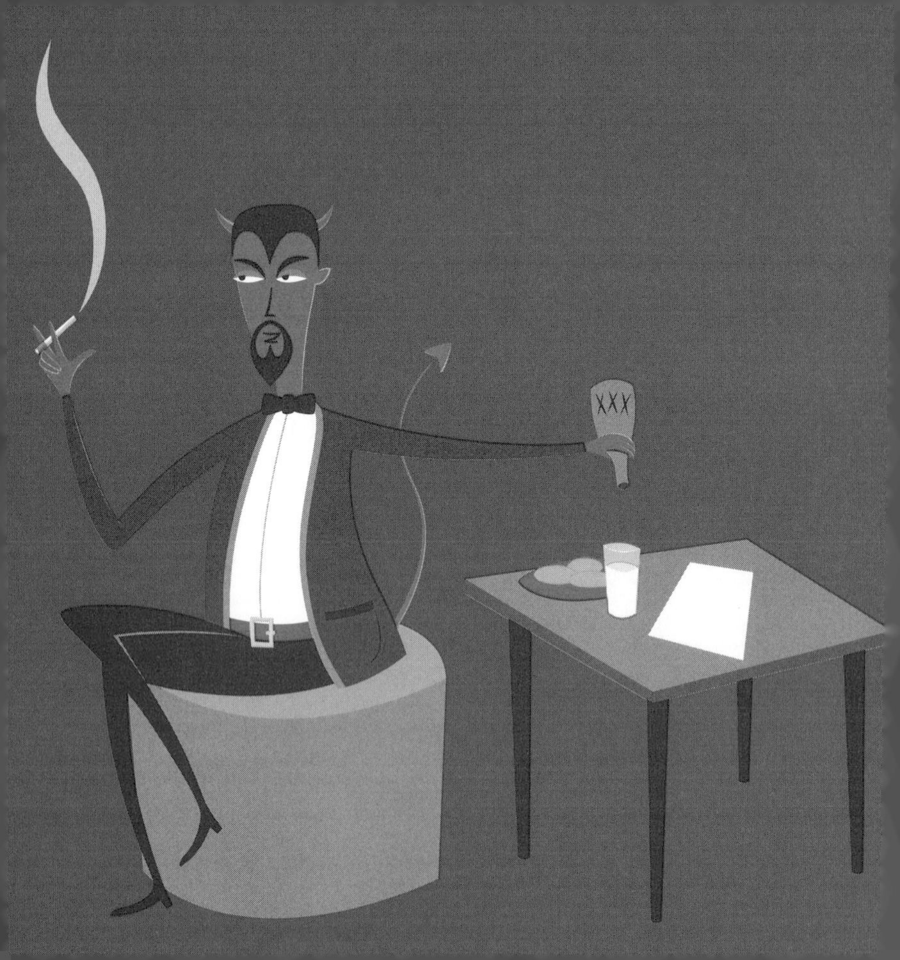
XXX

'Tis the season to be jolly.

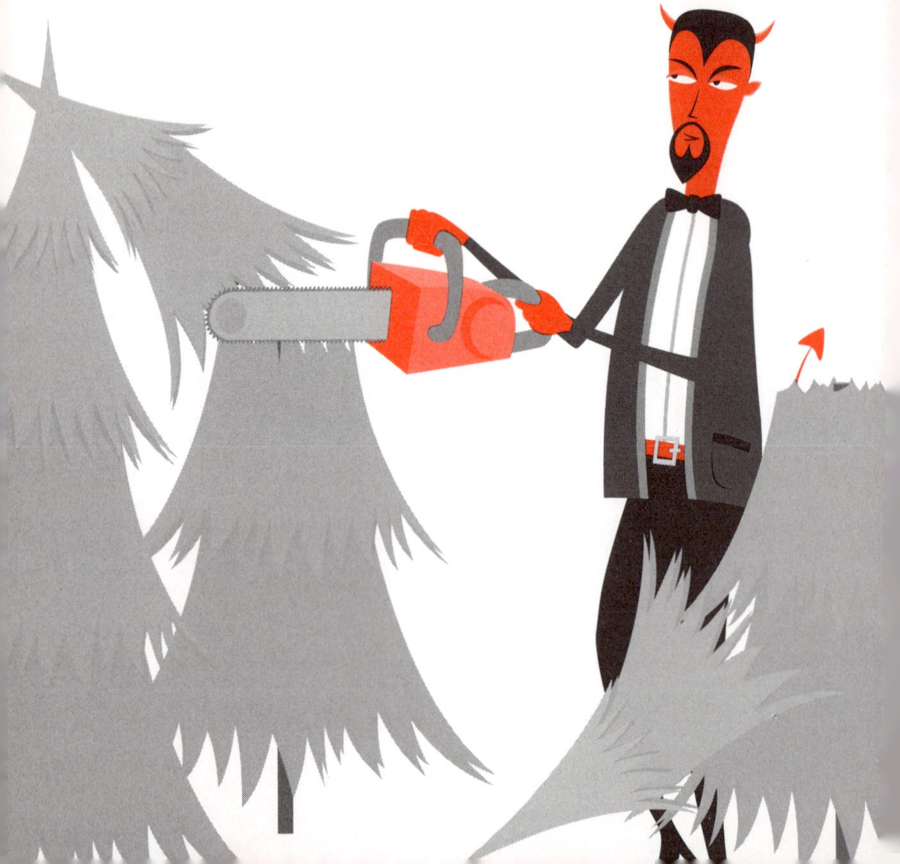

I just love to trim ✷ ✷ Christmas trees.

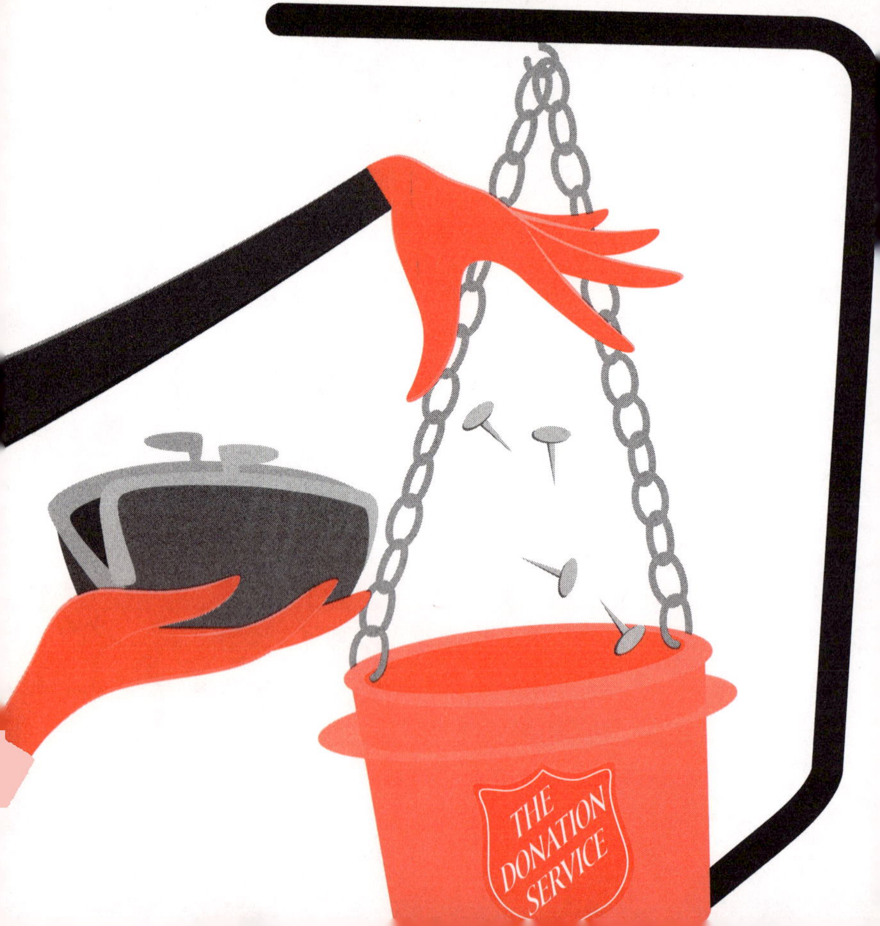
THE
DONATION
SERVICE

Yes, I'd like to make a difference.

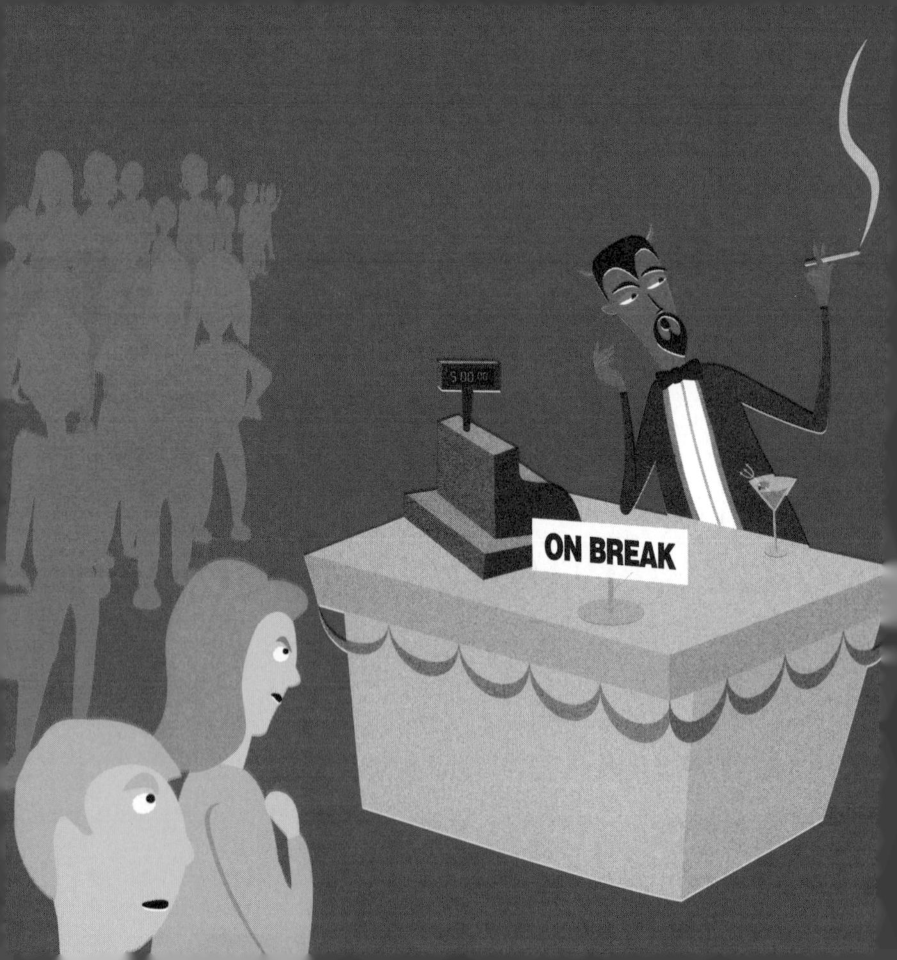
ON BREAK

All is calm?

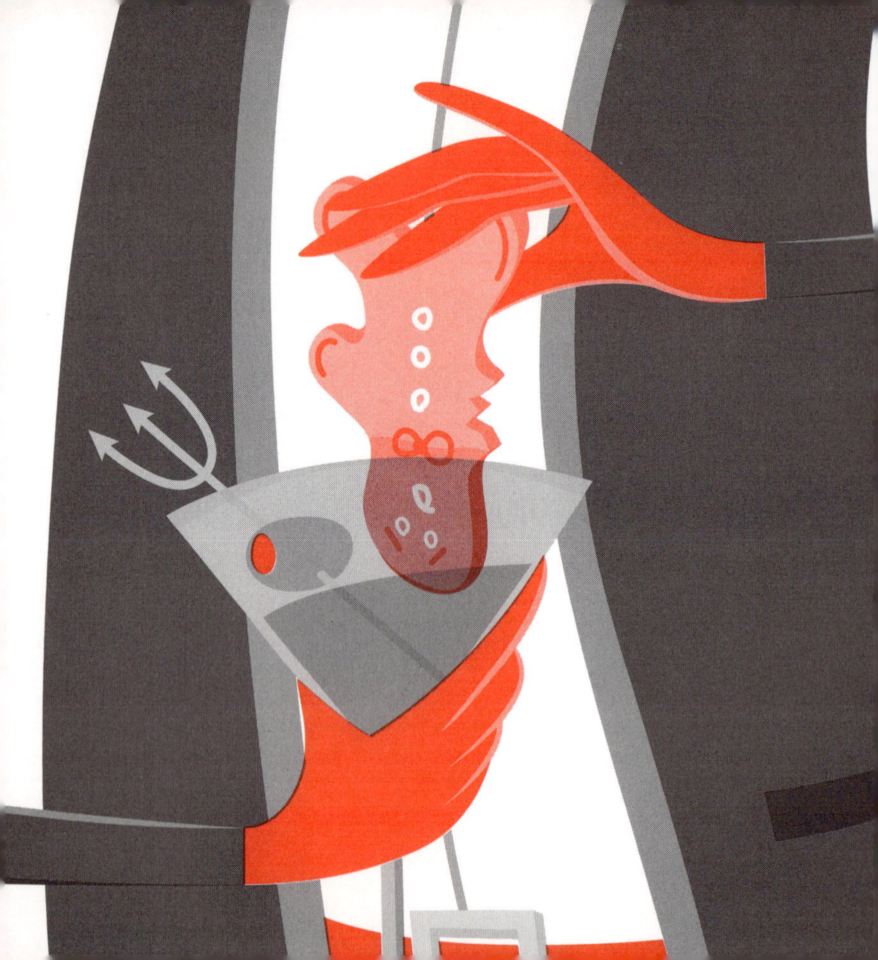

Dunk and disorderly.

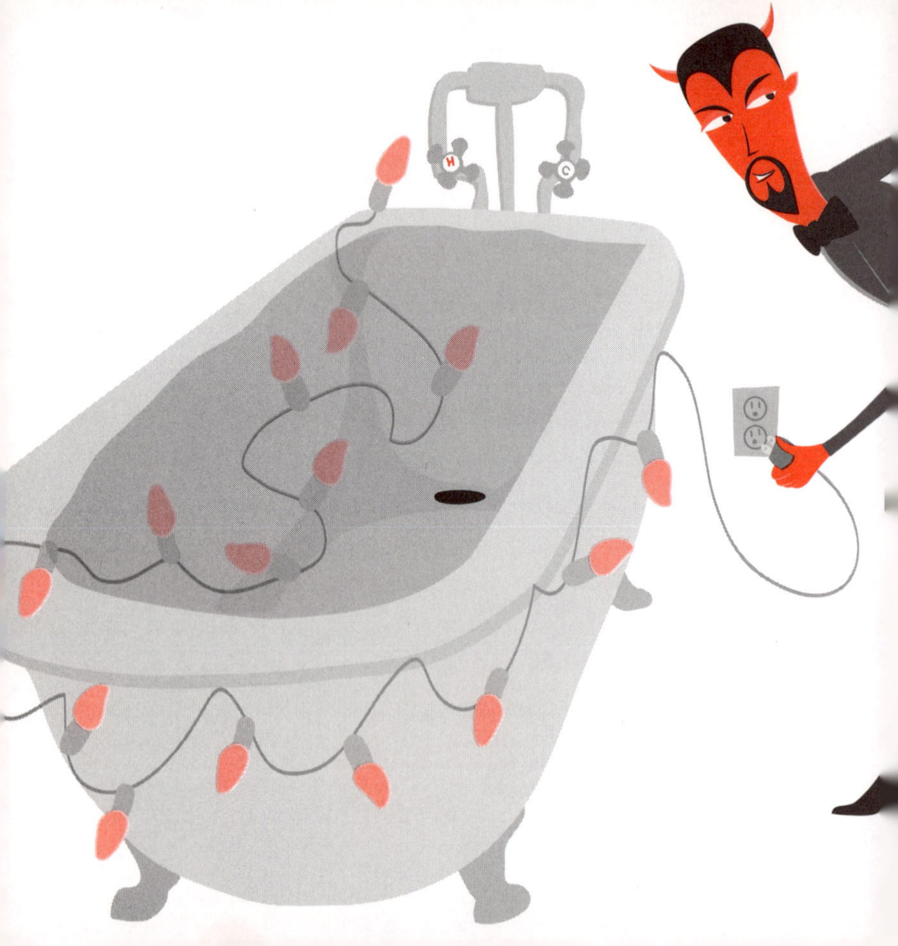
H
C

In the air there's a feeling of Christmas.

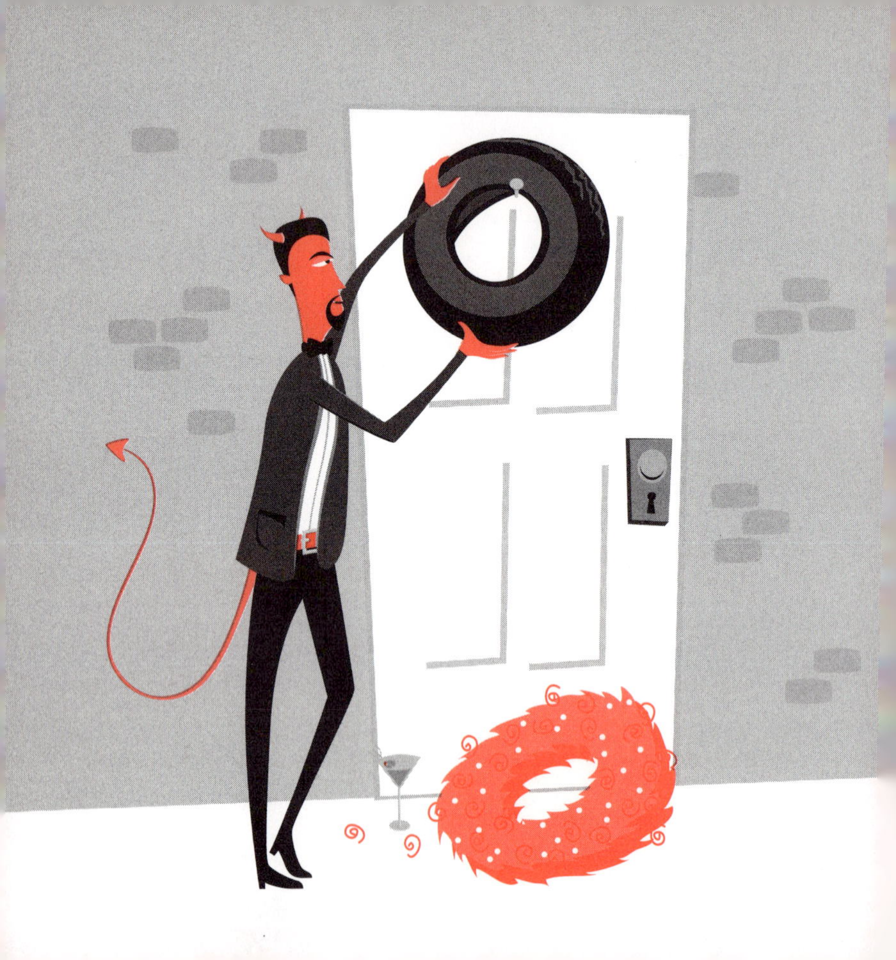

Tired of the holidays?

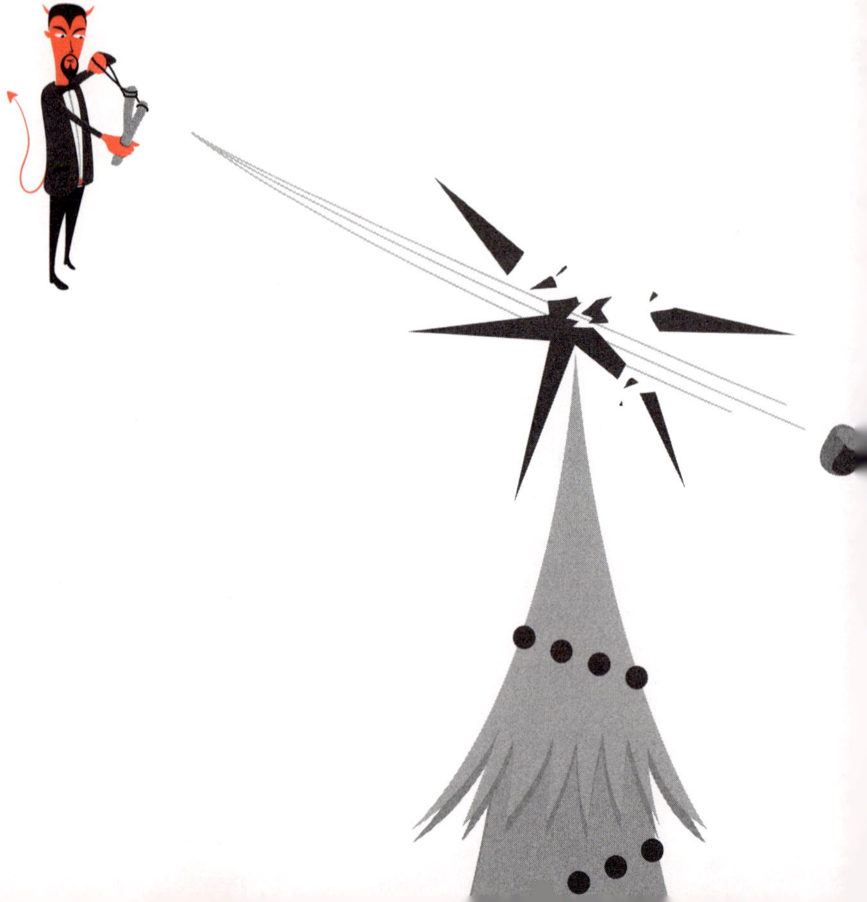

First star I see tonight.

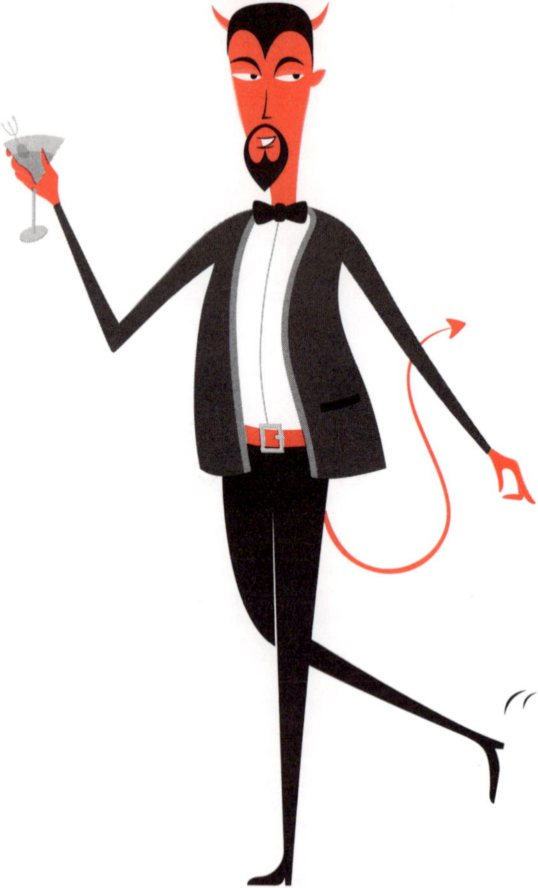

Let's kick some glass!

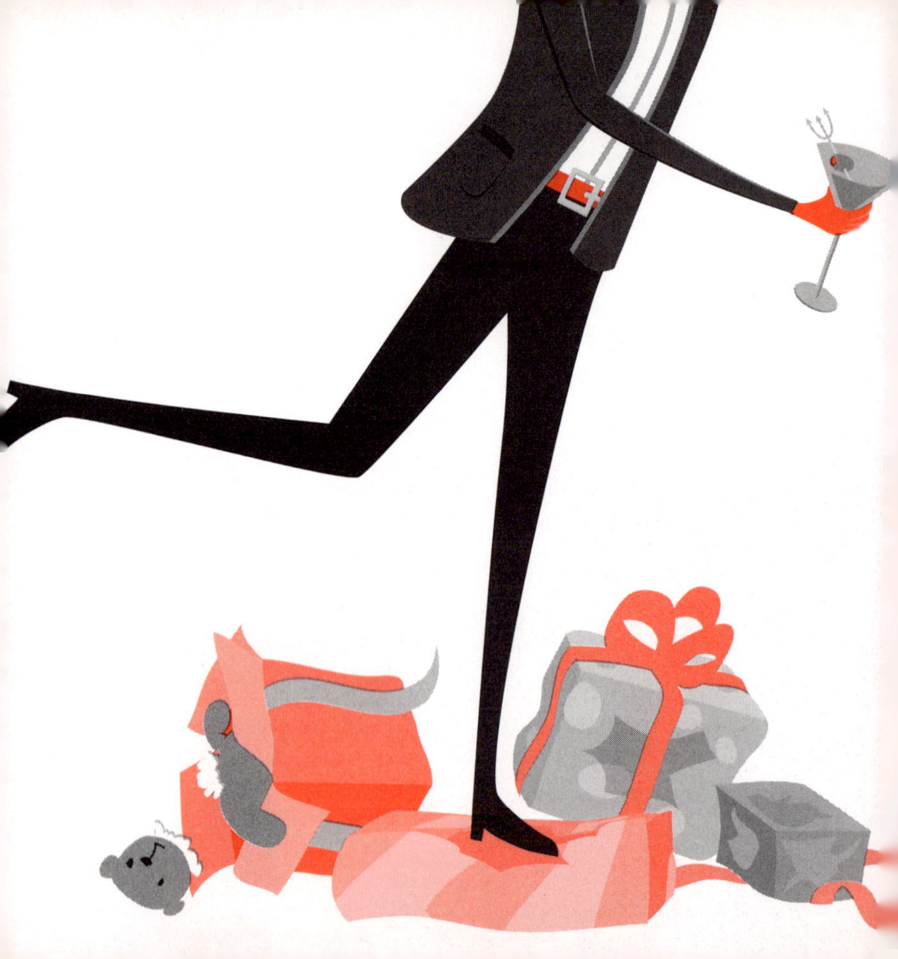

Smashing, absolutely smashing.

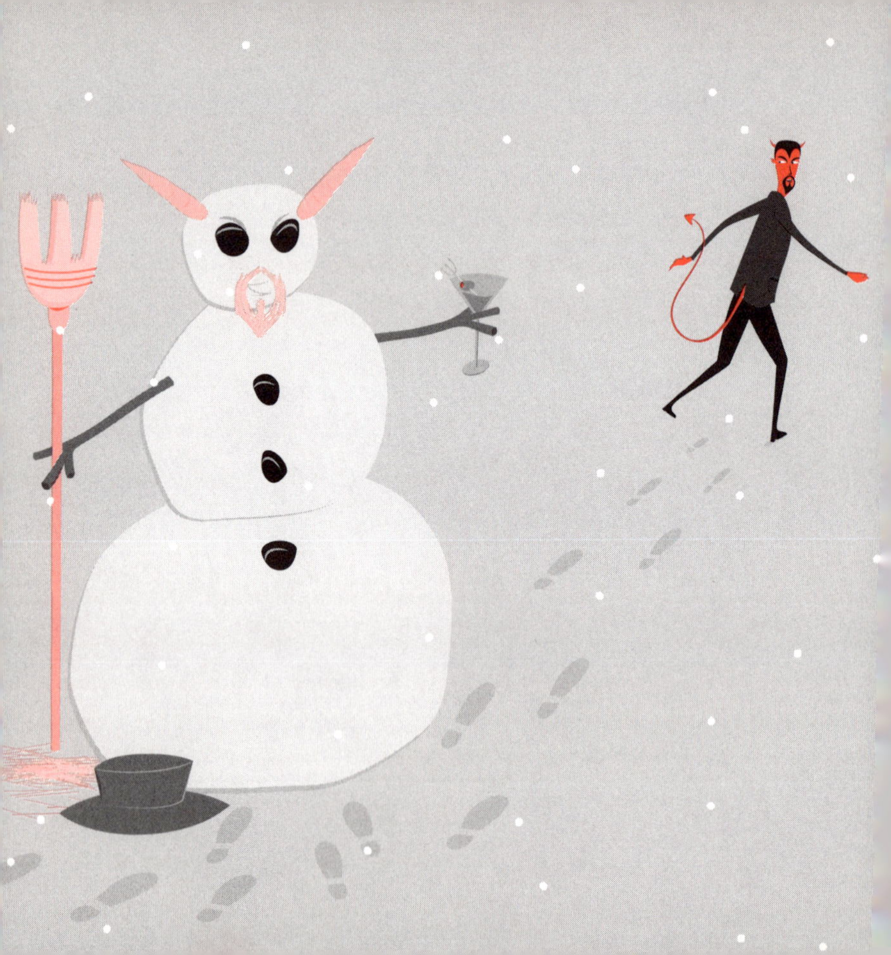

In the meadow
we will build a snowman.

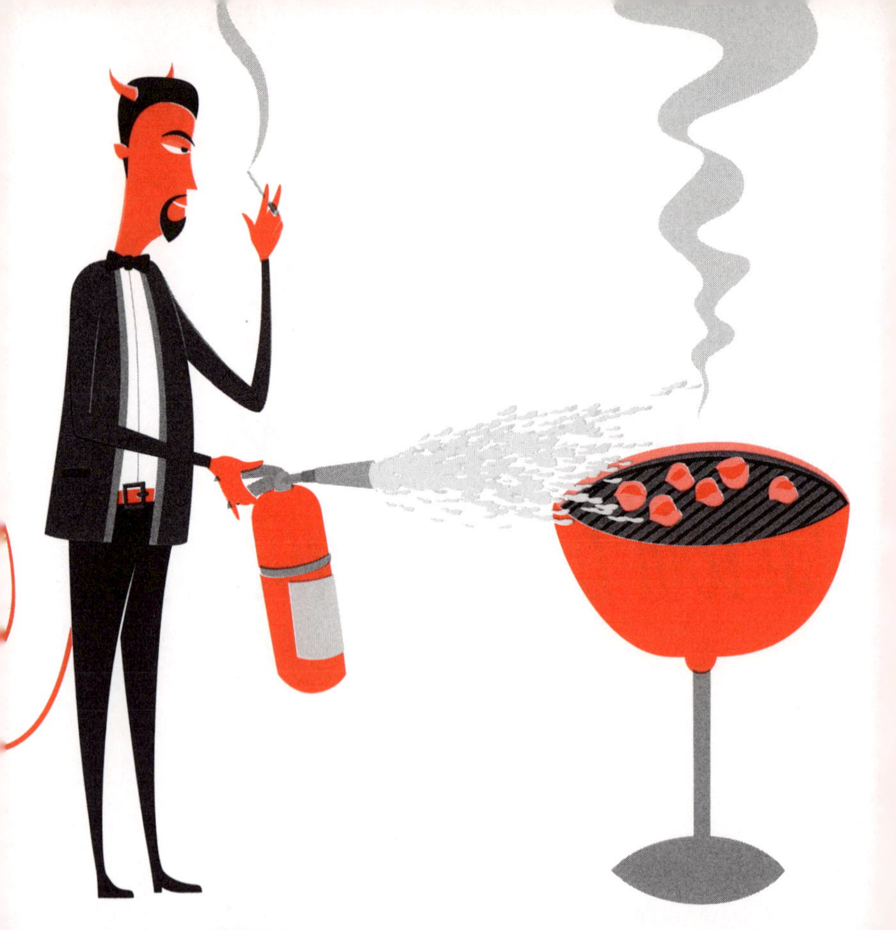

Roasting on an open fire? Not.

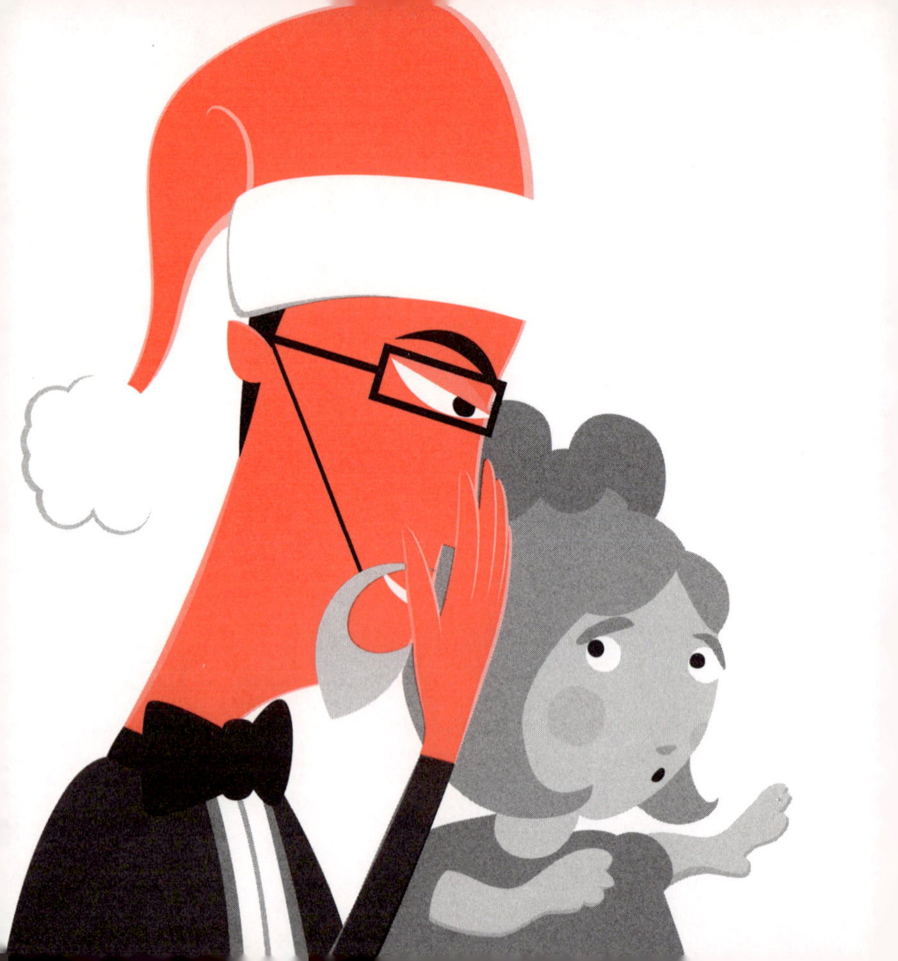

We're all out of toys this year.

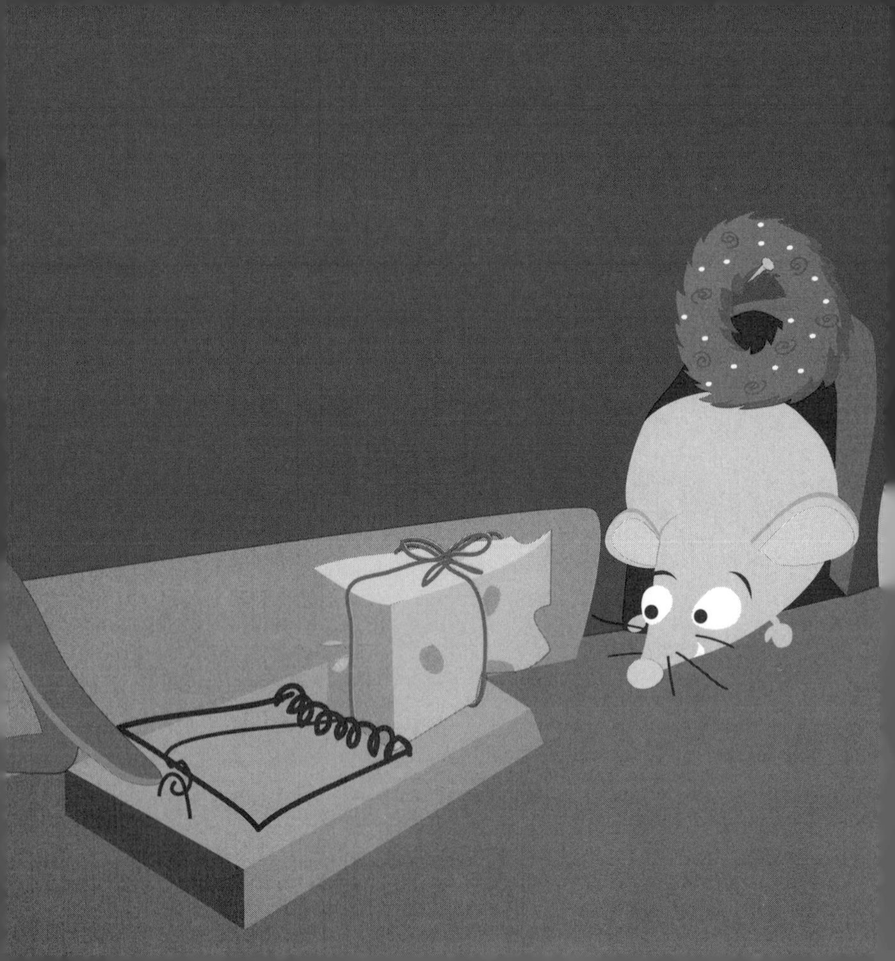

* Not a creature was stirring. *

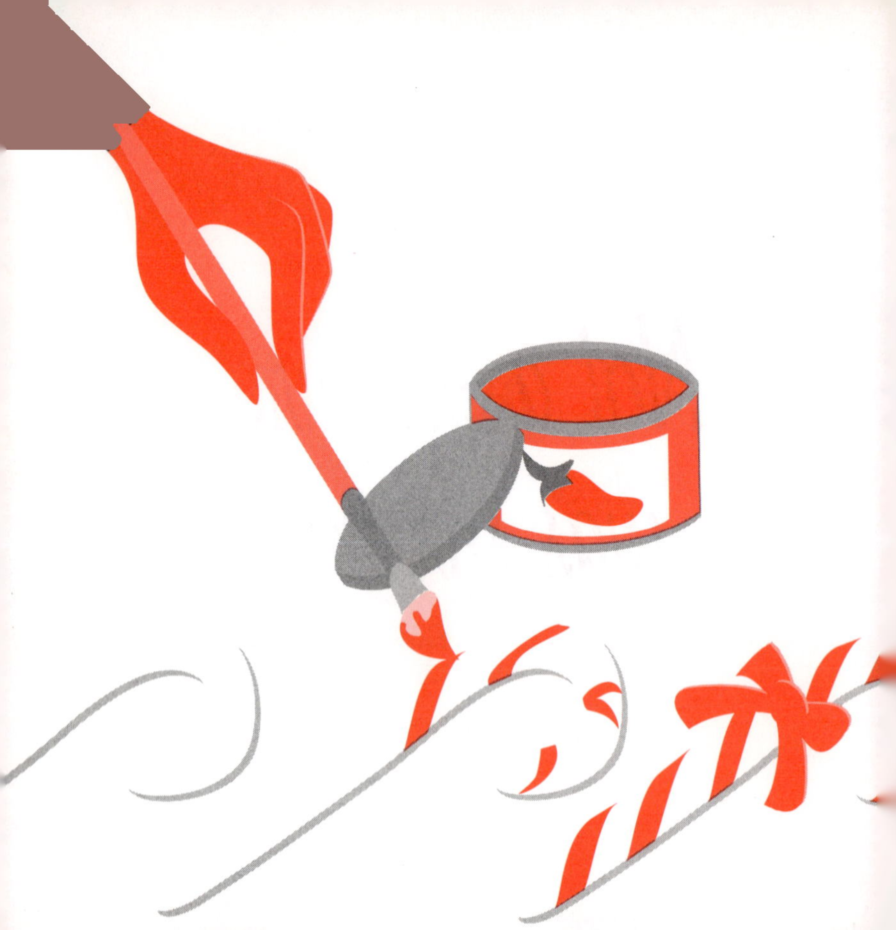

Holiday treats, with a twist,

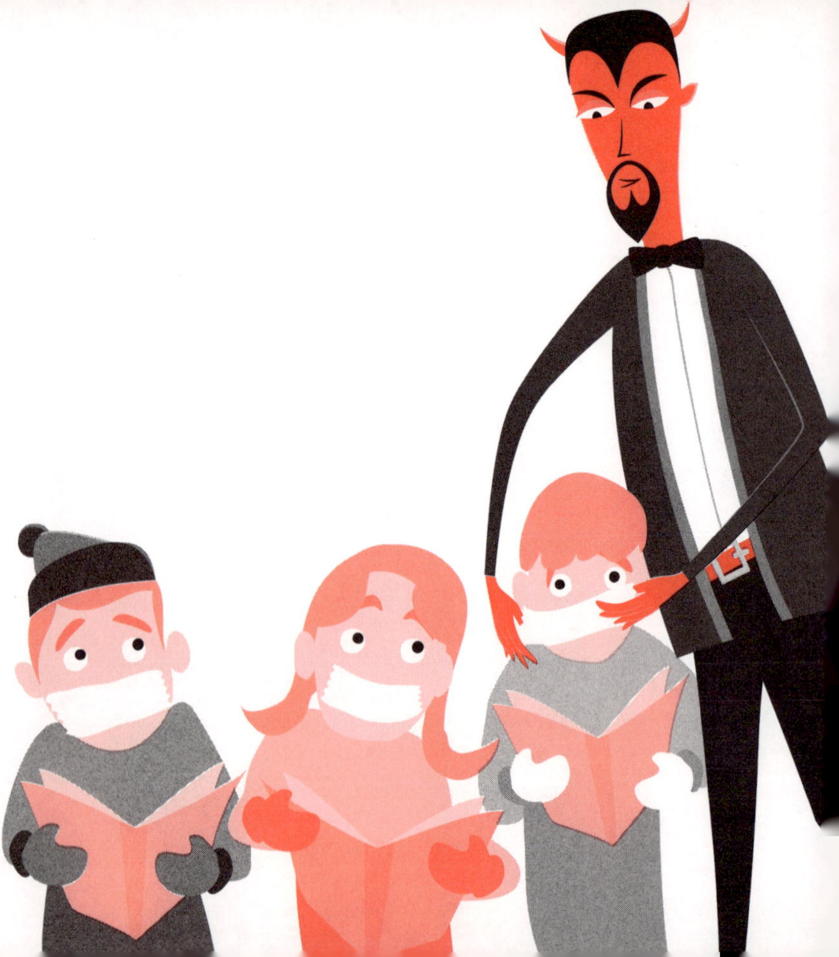

Silent night, my favorite. *

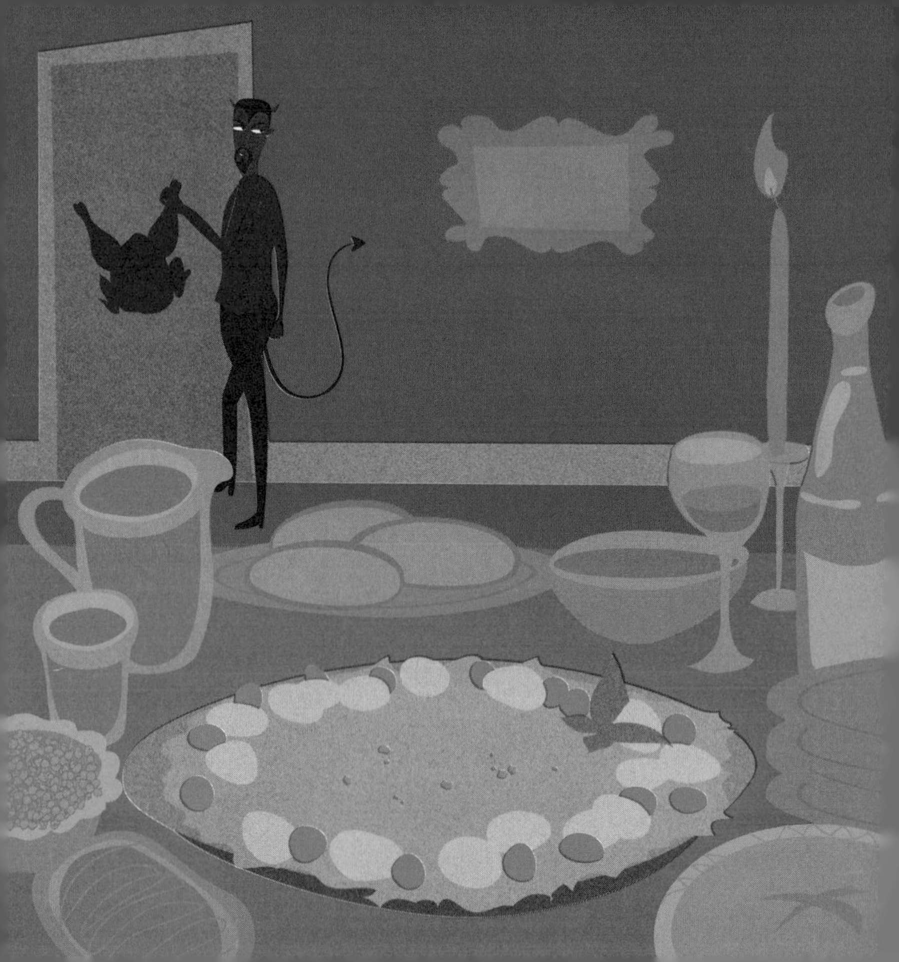

No tidings of comfort or joy.

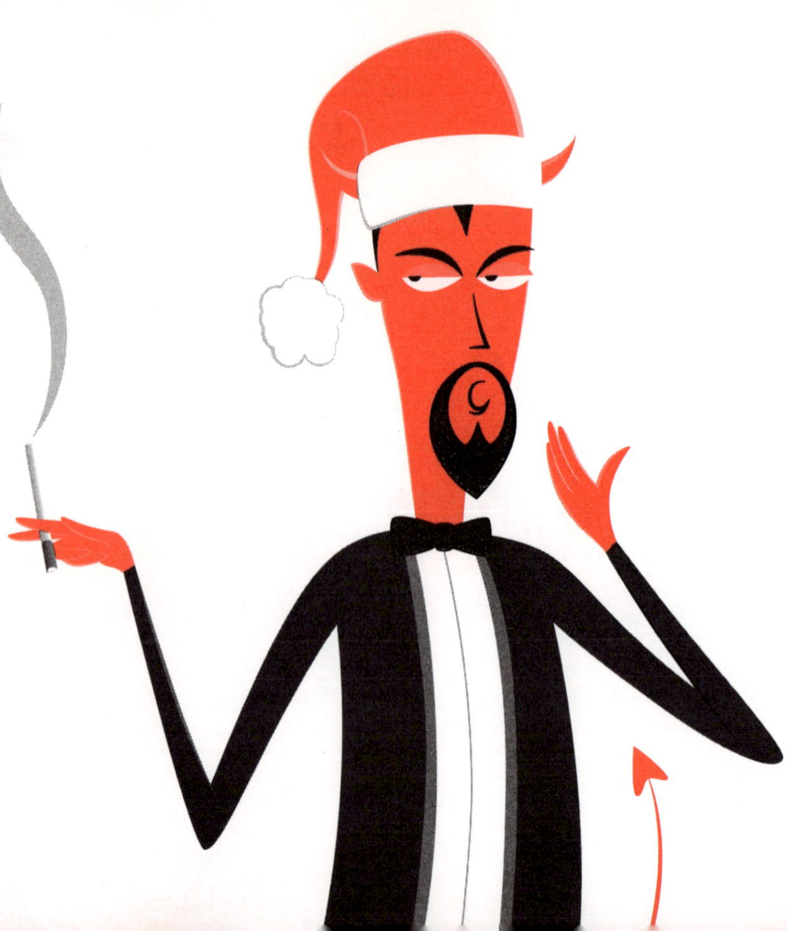

Ho ho hum.

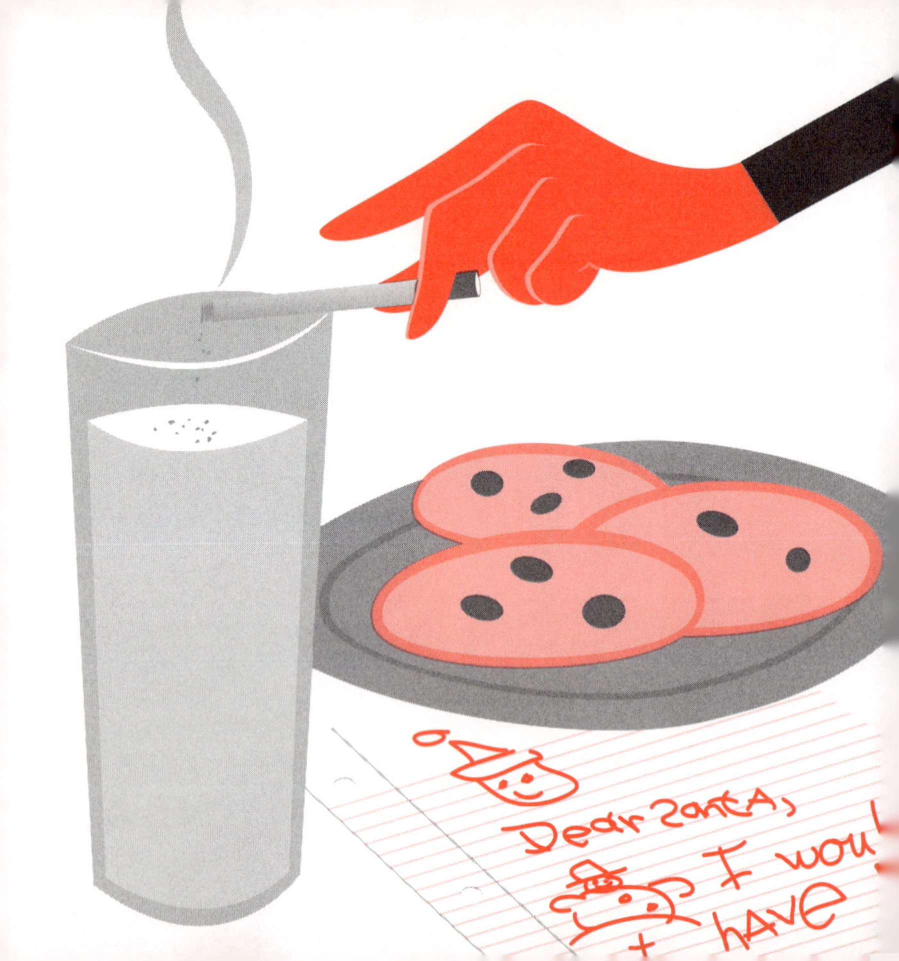
Dear Santa,
I wou
have

He's fat anyway.

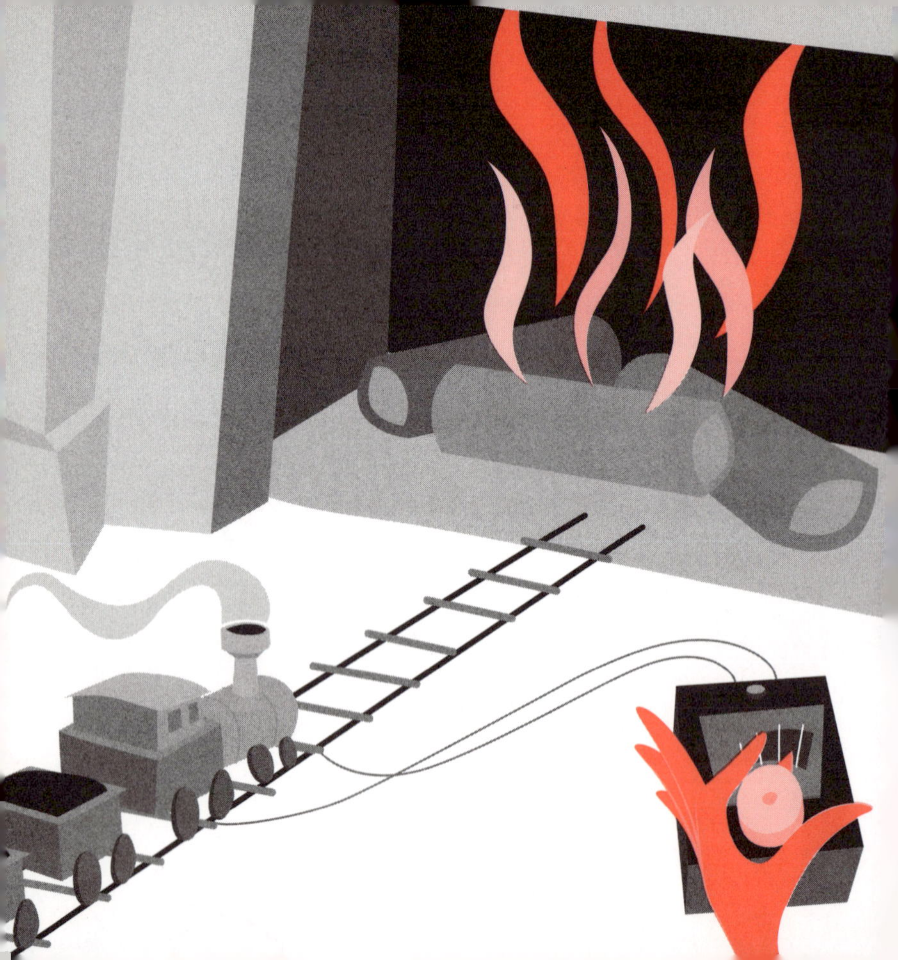

Laughing all the way.

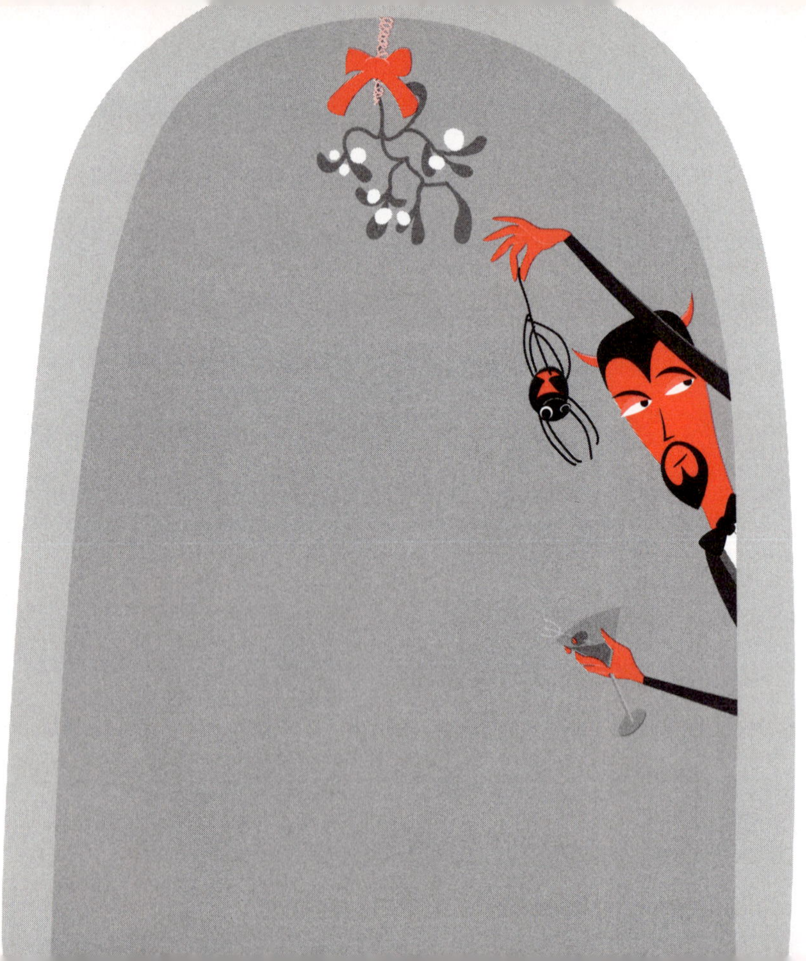

Holiday kisses.

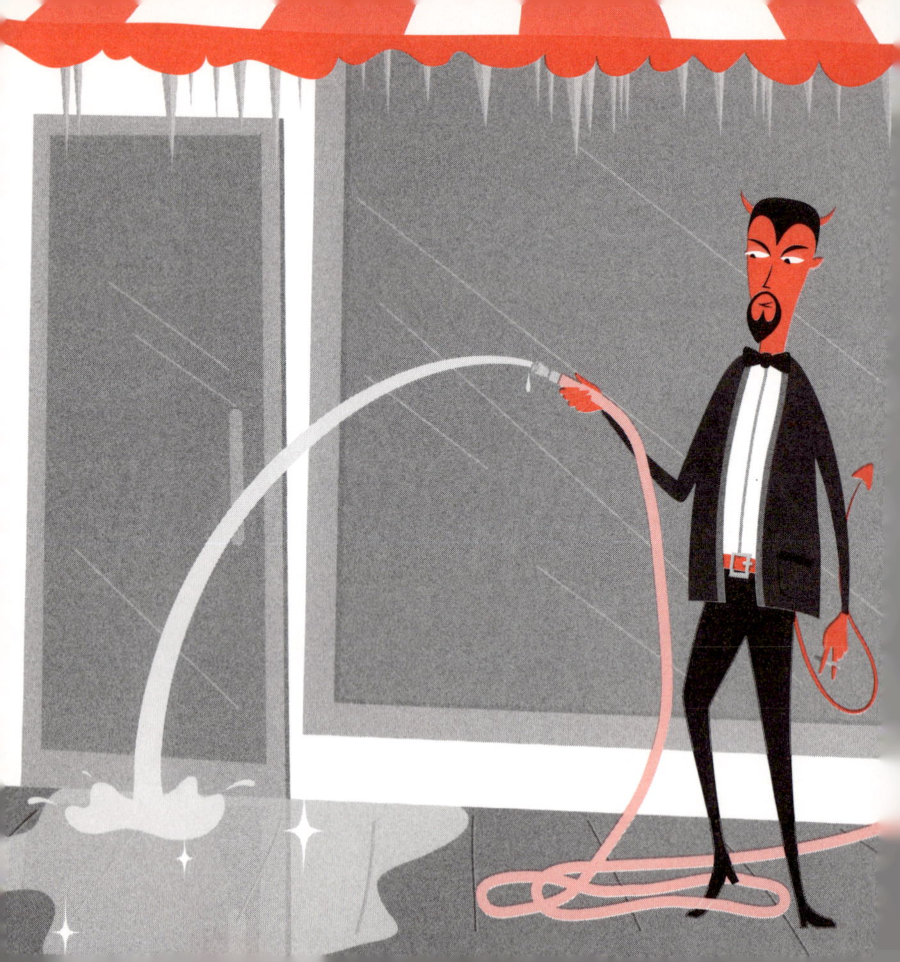

All is glistening.

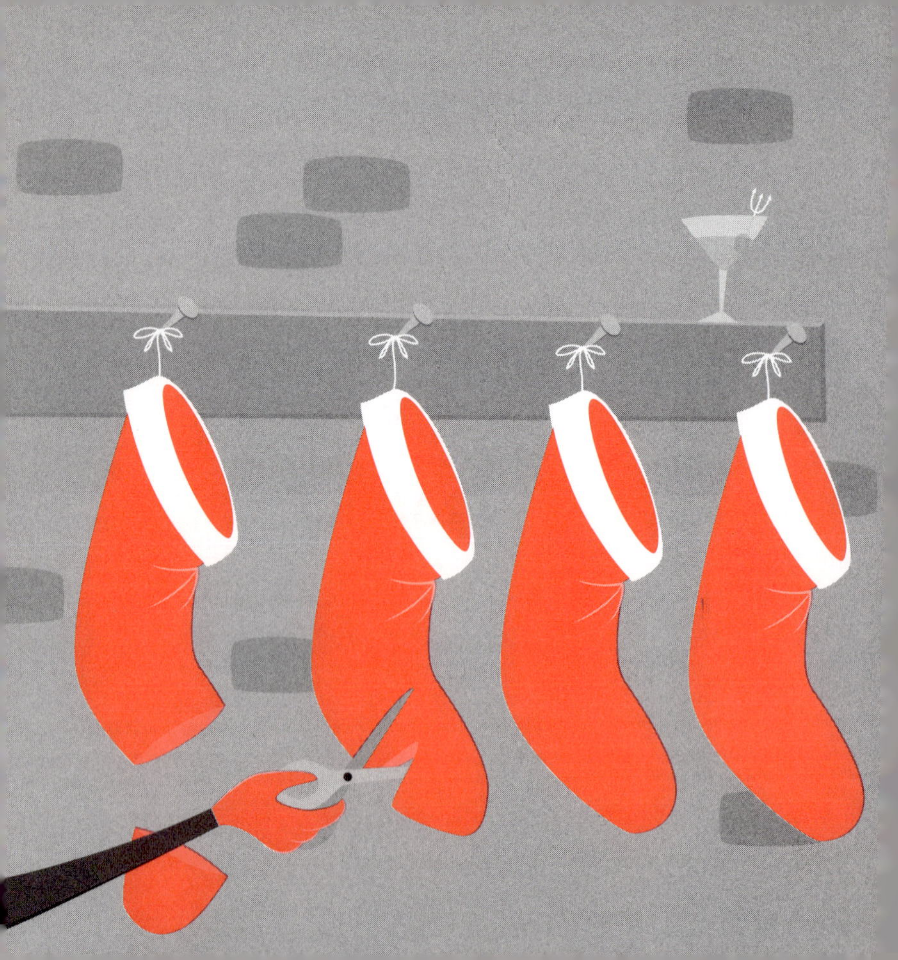

By the chimney with care.

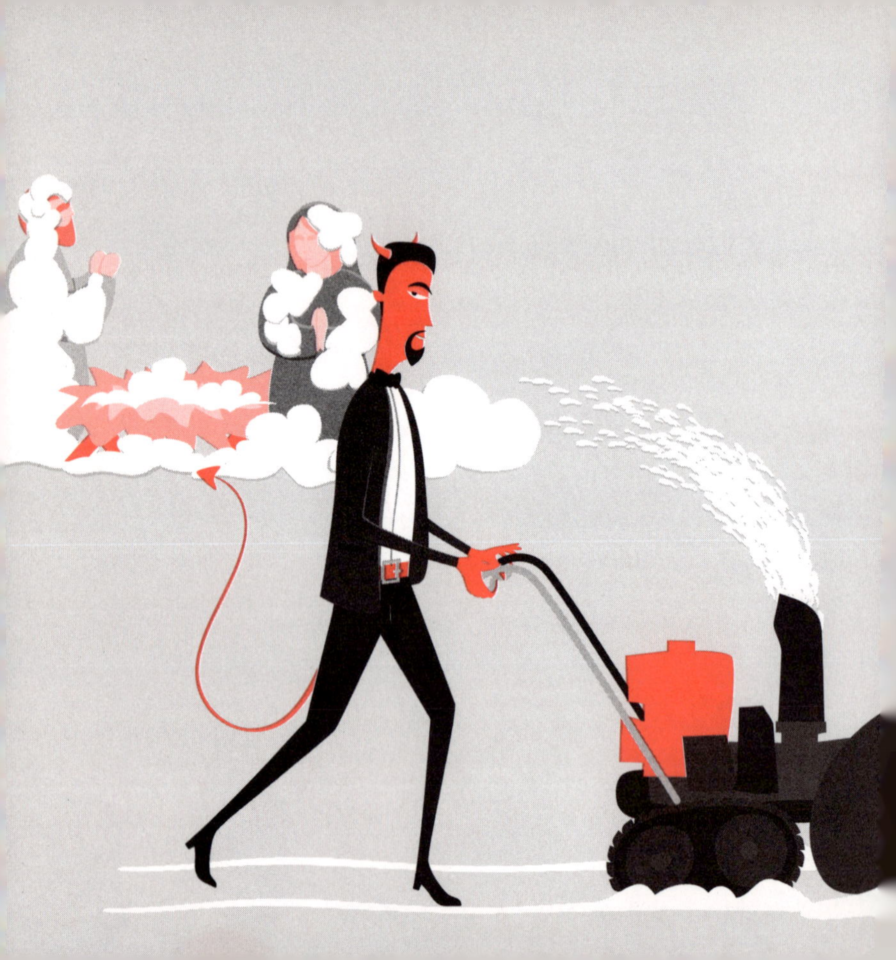

Let it snow, let it snow, let it snow.

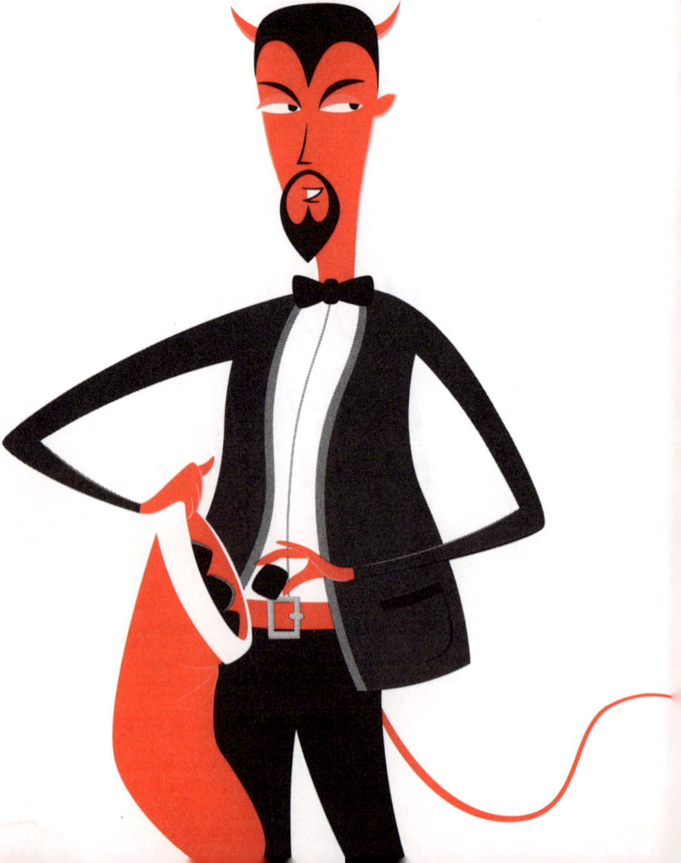

Season's greetings.

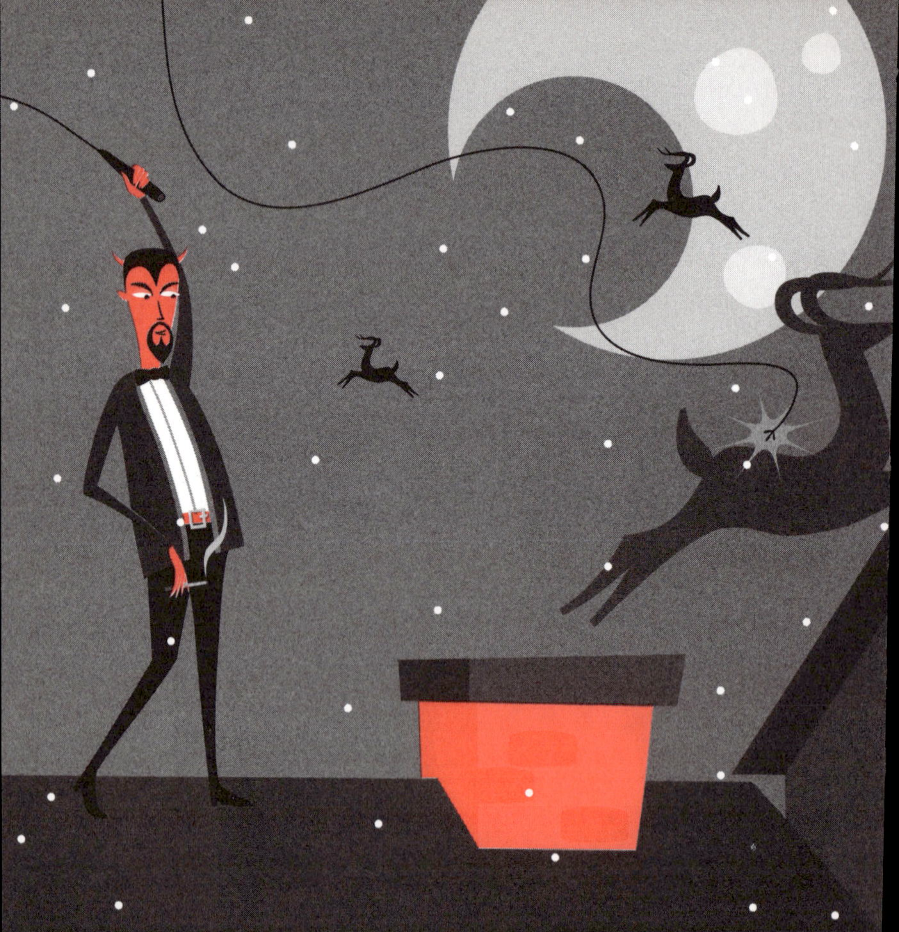

And who will guide the sleigh tonight?

PHOTOS WITH
SA TA N
AT THE MALL
OPEN
MON -THURS
HOURS
10 30 AM - 3 00 PM
SAT SUN 1AM- 5PM

There's been a change.

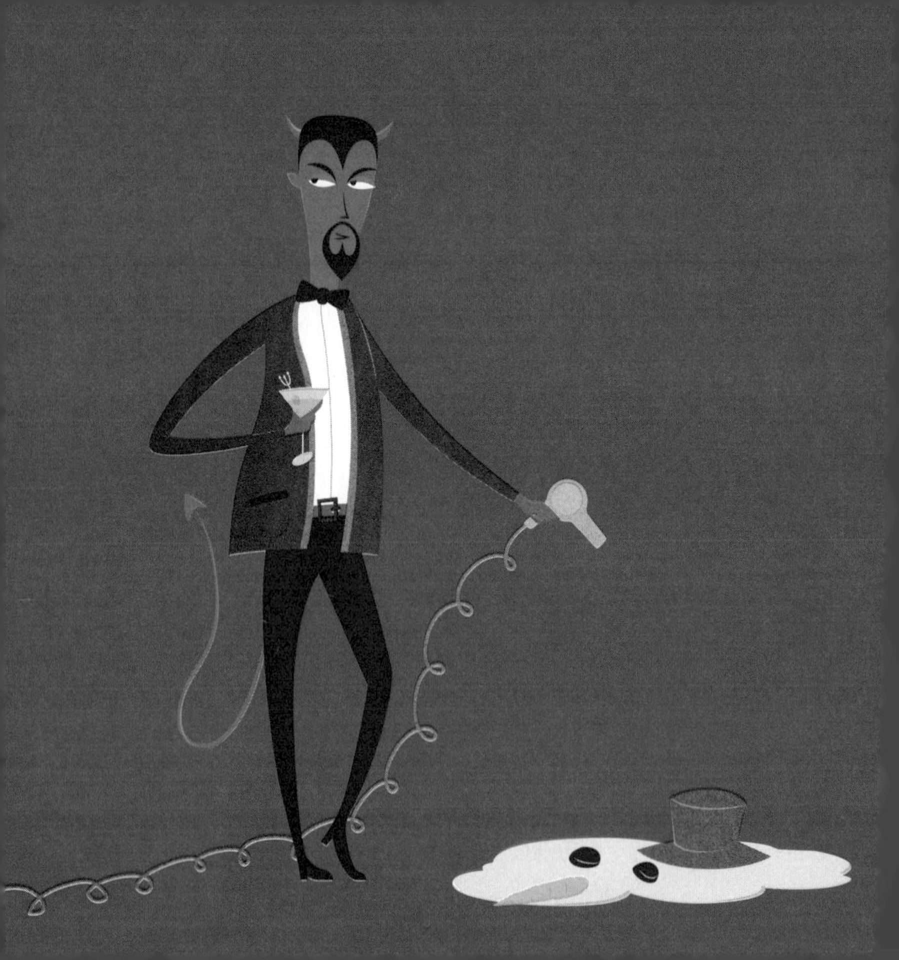

Warm wishes.

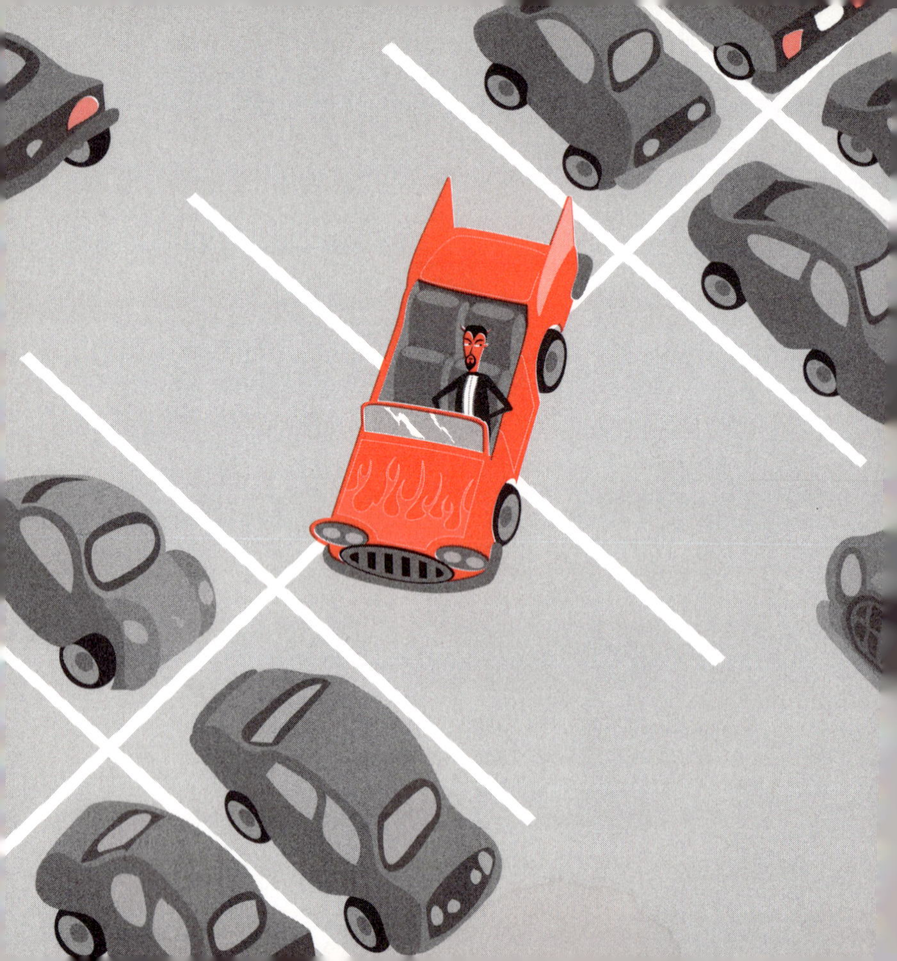

Fa la la la la.

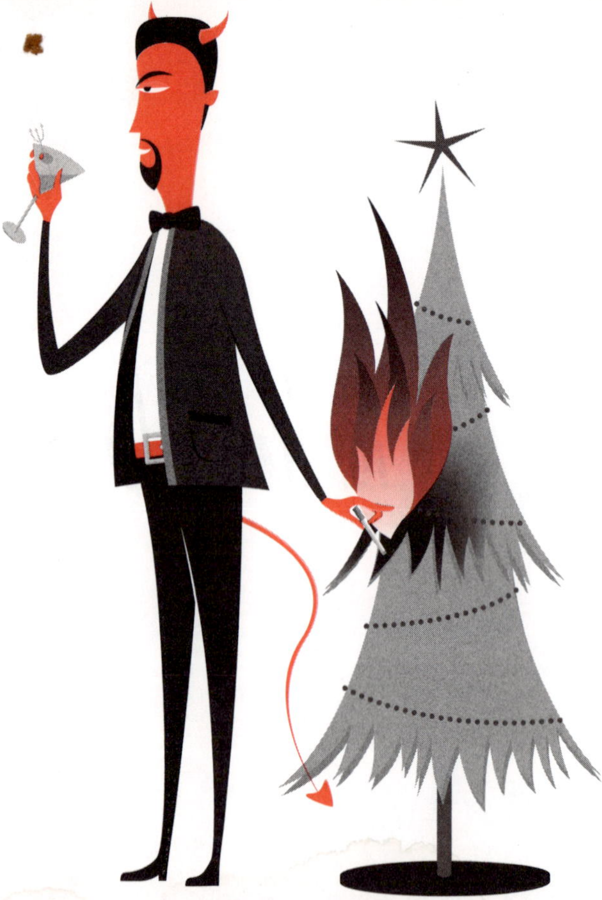

And may all your Christmases be bright.

Acknowledgments

Unpleasant thoughts like the ones collected in this book are rarely conceived in solitude. I particularly want to spread the shame to Aaron Thompson and Bradley Smith for their degenerate collusion. Joel (last name purposefully not disclosed), I hope your family forgives you. Rhonda, Maryanna, Armando, Mike, and the rest of you, you'll get what you deserve.